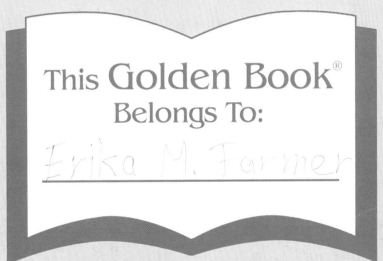

This Golden Book®
Belongs To:

Erika M. Farmer

About the Characters

Snow White

Snow White is a lovely young princess. Despite her royal role, she is forced by the wicked queen, her stepmother, to dress in rags and work as a scullery maid. Even so, Snow White remains gentle and graceful. Her charm and sweetness attract everyone but the jealous queen and ultimately lead the Prince — as well as the Seven Dwarfs — to be enchanted by her.

The Prince

A strapping and handsome young man, the Prince is consumed with love at first sight upon gazing at Snow White. Riding on his pure-white steed, he is a strong but not overbearing man. With one tender kiss to his true love, he magically transforms Snow White, waking her from her otherwise endless sleep.

The Queen

The vain and wicked queen is quick to anger and vengeful. Beautiful in a haunting way, she is also frighteningly evil. Her true wickedness shows through when she disguises herself as an old hag and tricks Snow White. Eventually the Queen's nastiness catches up with her when, through the power of love, good once again overcomes evil.

The Dwarfs

Although small in size, the Seven Dwarfs — Happy, Doc, Dopey, Grumpy, Bashful, Sleepy, and Sneezy — have giant hearts. Overall, they are cheery (except for Grumpy), charming, and fiercely loyal to Snow White. Though usually found in a group of seven, the dwarfs are quite individual, each with his own defined personality and amusing traits.

My Favorite Sound Story™

Walt Disney's Snow White and the Seven Dwarfs

GOLDEN BOOKS
Golden Books Publishing Company, Inc., Racine, Wisconsin 53404

ELECTRONIC UNIT MANUFACTURED IN CHINA.

Adapted by Laura Rossiter
Illustrations by Robbin Cuddy

Once upon a time, there lived a lovely princess named Snow White. She lived in a grand castle with her wicked stepmother, the Queen. More than anything else, the Queen feared that Snow White would grow up to become more beautiful than the Queen herself. Full of jealousy, she treated Snow White cruelly, dressing her in rags and forcing her to work as a maid.

Every morning, Snow White awoke with the **BIRDS.**  One

morning, as she went about her work singing and **LAUGHING,**

a handsome prince appeared. He had been watching Snow White and had

fallen in love with her.

From a window, the Queen was watching, too. Angrily, she turned to her

magic mirror and chanted a **SPELL.**  "Magic mirror on the wall,

who is the fairest one of all?"

"Alas," the mirror replied, "Snow White is more fair than thee."

HEIGH-HO and off we go!

The Queen ordered her huntsman to kill Snow White. The huntsman

took the Princess deep into the forest. As they walked, Snow White

LAUGHED and called to the **BIRDS.**  Suddenly, the

huntsman drew his knife. But he couldn't bring himself to hurt her.

"Forgive me!" he cried. He told Snow White what the Queen had ordered and begged her to run away. Then he returned to the Queen and told her that the deed had been done. The Queen **CACKLED.**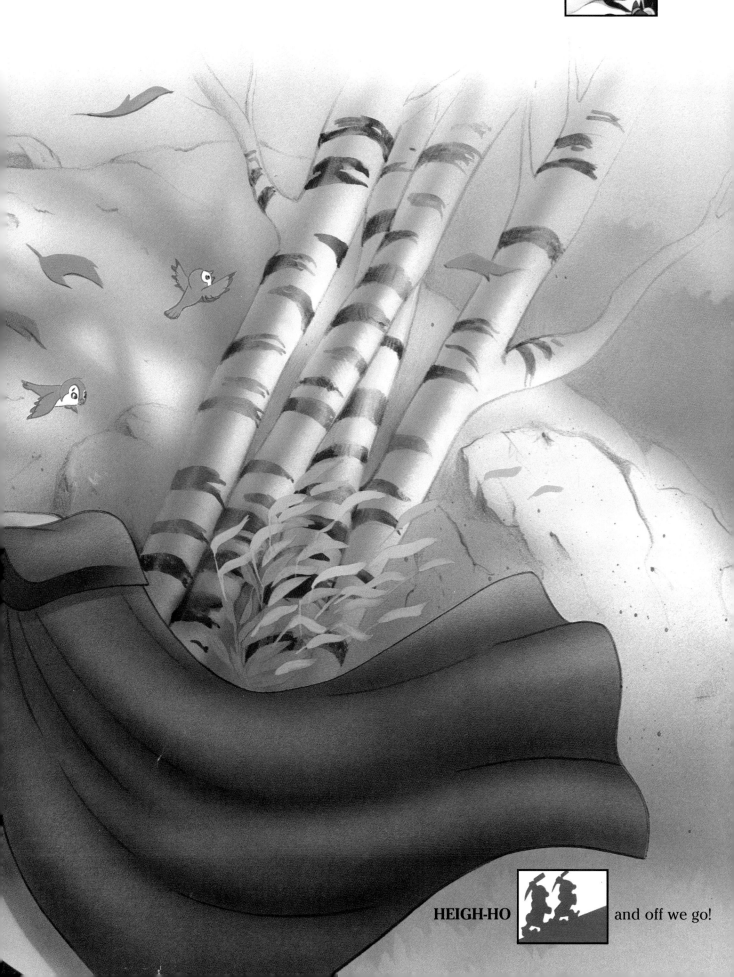

HEIGH-HO and off we go!

But deep in the woods, the **BIRDS**  led Snow White to a strange little cottage.

"Hello!" she said, stepping inside. The cottage was a mess! "Maybe if I clean the house, they'll let me stay," she said to the **BIRDS.** With help from the forest animals, she set to work at once.

Upstairs, Snow White **LAUGHED** when she found seven little beds, each with a name carved into it: Doc, Happy, Sneezy, Dopey, Grumpy, Bashful, and Sleepy.

"I'm a little sleepy myself," she yawned to the **BIRDS.**  And with that, she lay down and fell asleep.

HEIGH-HO and off we go!

Meanwhile, at a diamond mine nearby, the Seven Dwarfs had finished a hard day's work. At Doc's **CALL,** they gathered their shovels and

PICKS and headed home.

To their **SURPRISE,** they found their cottage spotless.

And **TIPTOEING** upstairs, they found yet another

SURPRISE! A strange shape lay under the covers.

"Why, it's a girl!" exclaimed Doc.

"She's beautiful," Bashful **SMILED.** "Just like an angel."

HEIGH-HO and off we go!

Snow White woke up and looked at the **SMILING** dwarfs.

"How do you do?" she asked, greeting each dwarf by name. She introduced

herself and told the dwarfs what the Queen had planned. The dwarfs were

SURPRISED  by everything Snow White had been through and

invited her to stay.

HEIGH-HO  and off we go!

At the castle, the Queen stood before her mirror and recited the

SPELL.  "Magic mirror on the wall, who is the fairest one of all?"

The mirror answered, "In the cottage of the Seven Dwarfs dwells Snow

White, the fairest one of all."

"I've been tricked!" the Queen **CACKLED.**  Quickly chanting

another **SPELL,**  she changed herself into an old woman. Then

dipping an apple into a potion, she **CACKLED,** "One taste of

this poisoned apple, and Snow White's eyes will close forever."

HEIGH-HO and off we go!

That night, Snow White and the dwarfs sang and danced. Then, as

Snow White sat down **LAUGHING,** the dwarfs gathered around

her. She told them a story about a handsome prince. The dwarfs were

SURPRISED 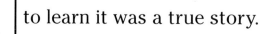 to learn it was a true story.

The next morning, the dwarfs arose at Doc's **CALL.**  They

gathered their shovels and **PICKS**  and said good-bye to Snow

White. Then, whistling a merry tune, the dwarfs marched off to work.

HEIGH-HO and off we go!

Disguised as the old woman, the Queen **TIPTOED**  through the forest to the dwarfs' cottage. There she found Snow White alone with the

BIRDS.  She greeted Snow White and held out the apple.

"This is a magic wishing apple," the woman **CACKLED.**  "One

bite will cast a **SPELL** 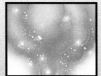 and make your dreams come true."

Snow White wished that her Prince would find her. She took a bite of the apple. In a moment, she was overcome by its evil **SPELL**  and fell to the floor.

The Queen **CACKLED.** "At last, I'll be the fairest in the land."

HEIGH-HO and off we go!

The **BIRDS** 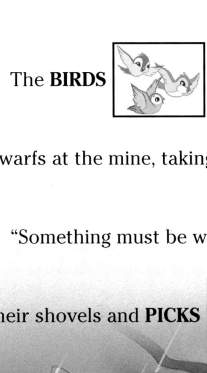 flew off to find help. They finally caught up with the

dwarfs at the mine, taking them by **SURPRISE**.

"Something must be wrong!" Doc **CALLED**.  The dwarfs dropped

their shovels and **PICKS**  and hurried back to their cottage.

A storm was brewing as the old woman fled the cottage. Suddenly, she

spotted the dwarfs heading home and climbed a rocky ledge to hide. As she

looked down, **CACKLING**  to herself, a bolt of lightning struck the

ledge, and she tumbled to her doom.

HEIGH-HO and off we go!

"Hurry!" Doc **CALLED.** The dwarfs ran as fast as they could to the cottage. They **TIPTOED** in and were heartbroken to find Snow White lying on the floor, very still.

But she was so beautiful that the dwarfs couldn't bring themselves to bury her. Instead, they built a glass coffin and kept watch over her, along with the BIRDS  and other animals of the forest.

HEIGH-HO and off we go!

One day, the Prince rode into the forest. Led by the **BIRDS,** he

soon found Snow White. He knew at once that she was the girl he had met by

the well. Sadly, he knelt and kissed her. To everyone's **SURPRISE,**

the kiss broke the evil **SPELL.** 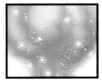 Snow White sat up!

"Look!" Bashful **SMILED**  as Snow White sat up. He, the other

dwarfs, and all the animals of the forest joined in joyful celebration.

With that, the Prince lifted Snow White onto his horse, and the two of them

rode off to his castle, where they lived happily ever after.

HEIGH-HO  and off we go!

SPOT THE DIFFERENCES

Look closely at the two pictures below, and you'll see that changes have been made to the lower picture. How many of the ten changes can you find?

TELL ME A STORY

Using your imagination, finish each of the stories below.

- As Snow White and the Prince ride off to his castle on the hill, they discover they are being followed. They hide in the woods to find out who is following them, and . . .

- One morning, as Snow White draws water from the well, she sees something unusual in the bucket. She is surprised to find . . .

Activity Pages

ANSWER ME THIS

Answer each of the questions below by looking back through the different pictures in the story.

1. How many white birds can you find throughout the story?
2. Count the number of deer you see in the story.
3. Who wears a crown in this book?
4. What color bows does Snow White wear in her hair?
5. How many times can you find the poison apple pictured in the story?
6. Count all the candles you find in the book. How many did you find?
7. How many of Snow White's raccoon friends can you find?
8. Which character in this book wears a feather in his hat?

SCAVENGER HUNT!

Look at the items below. Can you find each of these items pictured somewhere in the story?

BATTERY INFORMATION

BATTERY REPLACEMENT (See illustration below.)
Remove safety screw from battery drawer and pull drawer until it stops. Exhausted batteries are to be removed from the toy. Insert new batteries using any of the following brands (or an equivalent): • Duracell D303/357 • Eveready A76 • Maxell LR44. Make sure plus signs (+) are up as shown in the illustration. Batteries are to be inserted with the correct polarity. Supply terminals are not to be short circuited. Close the battery drawer and secure with safety screw. Do not use excessive force or an improper type or size of screwdriver. Retain book for future reference. Non-rechargeable batteries are not to be recharged.

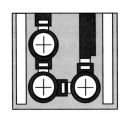

GENERAL SAFETY AND CARE
To ensure this product gives your family hours of enjoyment, please:
1. Inspect the unit to ensure battery compartment drawer is secured.
2. Prevent book and speaker opening from getting wet.
3. Do not expose book to excessive hot or cold temperatures.
4. Never use harsh chemicals to clean book. Wipe with a soft cloth dampened with water.

3.0-4.5 V DC
350 milliamps during use
3 x 1.5 V
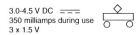

CAUTION

To ensure proper safety and operation, battery replacement must always be done by an adult. Never let a child use this product unless battery drawer is secured. Keep all batteries away from small children; batteries are small objects and could be ingested. Do not open battery, dispose of in fire, recharge, or put in backward. Only batteries of the same or equivalent type and rating as recommended are to be used. Do not mix new and used batteries or mix battery types. Do not mix alkaline, standard (carbon-zinc), or rechargeable (nickel-cadmium) batteries. DO NOT USE RECHARGEABLE BATTERIES.

REPLACEMENT BATTERY OFFER
To order replacement batteries for your Golden Books With Sound™ products,
send your mailing address along with a check or money order for $2.99 to:

Golden Books With Sound Products
Battery Replacement Offer
P.O. Box 1464
Wisconsin Rapids, WI 54495

Your replacement batteries plus a free screwdriver will arrive within 6 to 8 weeks.
This offer good only in the U.S. Price subject to change.